W9-ALN-186

WEST GA REG LIB SYS
Neva Lomason
Memorial Library
DISCARD

My Puppy Gave to ME

My Puppy Gave to Me

By Cheryl Dannenbring
Illustrated by Cynthia Kremsner

PELICAN PUBLISHING COMPANY
GRETNA 2014

Copyright © 2014
By Cheryl Dannenbring

Illustrations copyright © 2014
By Cynthia Kremsner
All rights reserved

The word "Pelican" and the depiction of a pelican are trademarks of Pelican Publishing Company, Inc., and are registered in the U.S. Patent and Trademark Office.

Library of Congress Cataloging-in-Publication Data

Dannenbring, Cheryl.
  My puppy gave to me / by Cheryl Dannenbring ; illustrated by Cynthia Kremsner.
       pages cm
  Summary: "In this cumulative rhyme based on 'The Twelve Days of Christmas,' a young child is a twelve-day recipient of puppy love, from eleven wrappings rumpled to the lights off the evergreen tree"--Provided by publisher.
  ISBN 978-1-4556-1943-6 (hardcover : alk. paper) -- ISBN 978-1-4556-1944-3 (e-book) [1. Stories in rhyme. 2. Christmas--Fiction. 3. Dogs--Fiction. 4. Animals--Infancy--Fiction.] I. Kremsner, Cynthia, illustrator. II. Title.
  PZ8.3.D237My 2014
  [E]--dc23
                           2014000009

Printed in Malaysia
Published by Pelican Publishing Company, Inc.
1000 Burmaster Street, Gretna, Louisiana 70053

My Puppy
Gave to Me

On the
1ST
day of Christmas,
my puppy gave to me . . .

t he lights off our
evergreen tree.

On the **2ND** day of Christmas,
my puppy gave to me . . .

two empty socks
        and the lights off our evergreen tree.

On the **3RD** day of Christmas,

my puppy gave to me . . .

three broken bulbs,
two empty socks,
and the lights off our evergreen tree.

On the **4TH** day of Christmas,
my puppy gave to me . . .

four fluffy friends,
  three broken bulbs,
two empty socks,
  and the lights off our evergreen tree.

On the **5TH** day of Christmas,
my puppy gave to me . . .

five pounds of love . . .

four fluffy friends,
   three broken bulbs,
two empty socks,
   and the lights off our evergreen tree.

On the **6TH** day of Christmas, my puppy gave to me . . .

six sloppy kisses,

**five pounds
of love . . .**

four fluffy friends,
three broken bulbs,
two empty socks,
and the lights off
our evergreen tree.

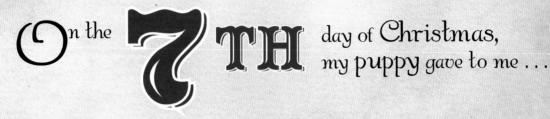

On the **7TH** day of Christmas,
my puppy gave to me . . .

seven missing mittens,
six sloppy kisses,

five pounds of love . . .

four fluffy friends,
three broken bulbs,
two empty socks,
and the lights off our evergreen tree.

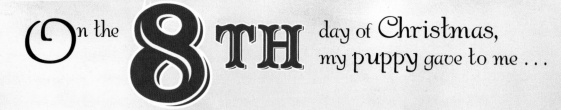

On the **8TH** day of Christmas, my puppy gave to me . . .

eight shredded ribbons,
seven missing mittens,
six sloppy kisses,

five pounds of love . . .

four fluffy friends,
three broken bulbs,
two empty socks,
and the lights off
our evergreen
tree.

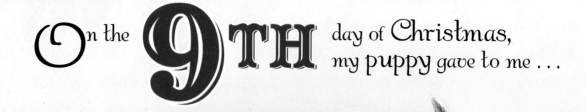

On the **9TH** day of Christmas, my puppy gave to me . . .

nine Santas jolly,
  eight shredded ribbons,
  seven missing mittens,
  six sloppy kisses,

five pounds of love . . .

four fluffy friends,
  three broken bulbs,
  two empty socks,
  and the lights off
  our evergreen tree.

On the **10TH** day of Christmas, my **PUPPY** gave to me . . .

ten sprigs of holly,
nine Santas jolly,
eight shredded ribbons,
seven missing mittens,
six sloppy kisses . . .

five pounds of love . . .

four fluffy friends,
three broken bulbs,
two empty socks,
and the lights off our evergreen tree.

On the 11TH day of Christmas, my PUPPY gave to me . . .

eleven wrappings rumpled,
  ten sprigs of holly,
nine Santas jolly,
  eight shredded ribbons,
seven missing mittens,
  six sloppy kisses,

five pounds of love . . .

  four fluffy friends,
    three broken bulbs,
  two empty socks,
    and the lights off our evergreen tree.

On the **12**TH day of Christmas, my PUPPY gave to me . . .

twelve cookies crumbled,
eleven wrappings rumpled,
ten sprigs of holly,
nine Santas jolly,
eight shredded ribbons,
seven missing mittens,
six sloppy kisses . . .

five pounds of love . . .

four fluffy friends,
  three broken bulbs,
two empty socks,

  and the . . .

lights off our evergreen tree.

Shhh . . .

My puppy gave to me

E DANNE   31057012039056

Dannenbring, Cheryl.

WEST GA REGIONAL LIBRARY SYS